What Does the Rain Play?

by Nancy White Carlstrom

illustrated by Henri Sorensen

Macmillan Publishing Company   New York
Maxwell Macmillan Canada   Toronto
Maxwell Macmillan International   New York   Oxford   Singapore   Sydney

For Gregory Hadrian Stormes
with love
—N.W.C.

To Anette and Nicolaj
—H.S.

When the sky is heavy as lead
and the whole world turns over, gray

and the little boy wears his coat with a hood
and boots that march him
right through the middle of puddles,

what does the rain play?

Rat-a-tat! Rat-a-tat! Rat-a-tat-tat-tat!

When the teacher reads stories full of sunshine
and everyone draws flowers and rainbows—
everyone except the little boy,

and the little boy sings and paints rain
and talks rain to the gerbils in their silver cage,

what does the rain play?

Tap tap trickle slide.

When the little boy walks home
up the steep steep hill
high above the bay,

and fog hides the bridge
    as boats rock in and out of mist,
what does the rain play?

Swish swish swiffle swish.

When the little boy gets home
and carries the drips inside
to his careful cat, Albert,
who purrs by his side,

and bread bakes in the oven,
    steaming up the kitchen windows
    the little boy writes his name on,

what does the rain play?

Tippita drippita tippita Jon.

When the little boy sets the table,
clanging the silverware,

pouring the milk,
and his father comes home
with tiny rivers running off his hat,

what does the rain play?

Clink clink gurgle drip!

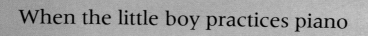

When the little boy practices piano

and his mother reads, and drinks tea
and his father sketches pictures
of the sailing trip they took last summer,

what does the rain play?

Plink plink! Sip sip! Slipper slip!

When the little boy crawls into bed
   and listens to the beat above his head;
it's dark
   and he's almost asleep and the roof begins to leak,

what does the rain play?

Ping! Ping! Ping in the pan on the bedroom floor.
Ping in the singing pan!

And the little boy says to his cat,
    the cat who has jumped up
    out of his deep snug-cat snooze,

"It's okay, Albert. Go back to sleep.
    The rain has played this song before."